the elf and the magic WINDOWS

A Christmas Fairy Tale

Ted C. Hindmarsh

ISBN 13:978-1-59955-179-1

Published by CFI, an imprint of Cedar Fort, Inc., 2373 W. 700 S., Springville, UT 84663
Distributed by Cedar Fort, Inc., www.cedarfort.com

LIBRARY OF CONGRESS CATALOGING-IN-PUBLICATION DATA

Hindmarsh, Ted C.
The elf and the magic windows : a Christmas fairy tale / Ted Hindmarsh.
p. cm.
Summary: Santa sends an odd little elf to the town of Golden Cove to teach the children a lesson about generosity.
ISBN 978-1-59955-179-1
[1. Conduct of life—Fiction. 2. Christmas—Fiction. 3. Elves—Fiction.]
I. Title.

PZ7.H56968El 2008
[E]--dc22

2008014864

Cover design by Angela Olsen

Typeset by Jennifer Boss

Printed in the United States of America

10 9 8 7 6 5 4 3 2 1

Printed on acid-free paper

On a lovely winter day not long ago, in a land not very far away, a small group of children lived happily with their families in a small village called Golden Cove that rested on a hillside between a thick forest and a beautiful mountain lake. Of course, some of the children lived more happily than others, but that's how it is in most villages.

It was Christmas Eve, and everyone was busy making goodies, wrapping packages, trimming trees, and otherwise decorating the entire village.

The sun was bright and the snow was deep and powdery, so the children put on their snowsuits. Some of them played fox and geese. They swooshed down steep hills on sleds and built big, white snowmen, which some of the other children knocked down.

When evening came they would all go to their snug homes and cuddle up in soft blankets around their cozy fireplaces where they would drink warm apple cider and eat donuts. Then they would go to bed early so Santa could come. It was wonderful to live in those days in Golden Cove. All of the children giggled and played. But some of them teased and were mean to each other. Although most of them were obedient and willingly shared, others disobeyed and kept everything to themselves. They were a trial for their parents.

As the children played in the snow, some of the grown-ups cut firewood and Christmas trees near the edge of the thick forest, and some of them stayed home to fix yummy dinners. They whistled and sang while they worked.

Suddenly, just as the sun reached the top of the sky, a quaint little man that nobody knew popped out of the thick forest and into the sunlight. He winced at the brightness as he looked about. Then he wobbled through the deep snow down toward the village. He looked so unusual that everyone stopped what they were doing and stared at him. Most of the villagers tried not to be impolite, but some of them giggled.

The strange little fellow had a big belly, small eyes, and a nose that was far too big for his face. He was dressed in a green coat that looked almost silly. It was tied with a rope about his middle. From that rope hung a large leather pouch that swung back and forth, bumping against his leg while he walked. He wore tan trousers, which were stretched much too tight and were stuffed into the tops of his brown leather shoes that turned up at the toes and curled.

A bright red feather stuck out of the band of a funny green cap that tipped to the side of his head and touched one of his large, pointed ears.

One of the little man's hands gripped a crooked walking stick, and the other held tight to a large canvas bag he had slung over his shoulder. The bag was bulging with strangely shaped bumps, and it seemed much too heavy for his spindly legs to hold up.

The little man didn't smile, but he didn't seem grumpy. He panted and wheezed from his work, and even in the cold air little beads of moisture stood out on his wrinkled forehead and glistened in the bright sunshine. Everyone privately thought that he looked like an elf!

Everyone wondered what sort of business would bring such a strange little fellow to Golden Cove. No one said "Hi," or "How do you do?" but as he passed they all followed.

Some of the children were concerned that he had to carry such a heavy load and wondered if they should offer to help, but they obeyed their parents' warnings to never get too friendly with strangers. Other children who thought only of themselves laughed and poked fun and even threw snowballs at him.

Their parents were embarrassed and couldn't make them stop, but the little man simply wouldn't be bothered. He didn't look right, and he didn't look left. He didn't speed up, and he didn't slow down. He didn't even yell, "Shoo!" or "Buzz off!"

Someone said they did hear him quietly grumble, but only a little.

Without hesitation the little man trudged into the village, right through the brightly decorated streets, until he got to the village square, just like he knew where he was going. Children and grown-ups were right behind him, causing such a commotion that everyone who was at home came out of their houses to see what was happening.

They all watched in amazement as he went to the square's center and plopped the big bag on the ground with a sigh of relief. It clanked and crunched as it hit the packed snow.

Without saying a word the little man unfastened the string that was tied about the opening of the bag. He reached in and rummaged around noisily. Finally he pulled out an object that looked like a big book but was made out of wood. He placed it on the snowy ground, and when he opened it there were startling snaps and pops as it unfolded, as if by magic, into a sturdy wooden box that was large enough for him and several other people to stand on.

Everyone gasped in amazement. The little man hopped on the box as if his legs were springs, and he stood there as if he were on a stage, right next to the big bag, which was still on the ground.

Again he reached into the bag and rummaged. The children and their parents watched carefully with wide eyes and tense muscles as they wondered what the strange little man would do next.

This time the little man pulled out a big hammer and placed it on the box at his feet. As he reached in again, his face twisted under the strain. He grunted as he pulled from the bag a big, brass bell that was so big he could hardly lift it. With effort, he held the bell up and struck it several times with the hammer as hard as he could.

Gong! Gong! Gong! Gong!

Then he dropped it to his feet with a clunk.

Some people, holding their ears, mumbled under their breaths that he didn't have to do that to get everyone's attention.

The same questions were in everyone's eyes and on everyone's faces and lips: who was this strange little man, and what was he doing?

As the excited crowd fell silent with the echoing tones of the bell, the little man spoke. As he did, it was clear that the surprises were only beginning. Not only did the man look strange, but he also talked strange too.

> "Hear ye, hear ye, village folk.
> Please gather all about!
> Now move in close and listen up,
> So I won't have to shout!
>
> "Grundlebumpkin is my name.
> My friends just call me Grundle.
> The reason that I'm here today
> Is to deliver this big bundle.
>
> "In the busyness of Christmas
> Santa couldn't come himself,
> So he sent me, his number one,
> Head honcho Christmas elf."

An excited murmur rumbled through the crowd. So, he *was* an elf! And he wasn't just any old elf; he was the most important of Santa's elves who had been sent on a special errand by Santa himself. The villagers wondered why he would be sent to Golden Cove, but no one asked. No one made a sound. No one hardly even breathed.

Grundle continued:

"I'm obviously in a rush,
So let's not waste a minute.
Let's talk about this heavy bag
And all the stuff that's in it.

"Santa says there're people here
Who need to learn some things.
So he's devised a little game
To see what good it brings.

"This is Santa's magic bag.
The fool thing weighs a ton!
The objects in it could bring joy
To nearly anyone.

"But there are other things in here,
It should be understood,
That would be fit for only those
Who haven't been that good.

"Like lumps of coal and dirty socks
And bits of broken glass,
And other kinds of junk that simply
Haven't any class.

"Now Santa's plan, you see, is this —
And trust me, there's a reason —
The kids from Golden Cove can't choose
Their gift from him this season.

"The gifts you children choose will go
To kids whose names are new.
And as you choose their gifts for them,
They'll choose your gifts for you."

The children and their parents looked at each other in surprise. Another murmur went through the crowd. Some of the children were excited, but some of them were angry.

"Now wait a minute," a snippy boy named Calvin piped up. "You mean to tell me that the only way I'm gonna get a gift from Santa

this year is if I pick one for someone else and they get to pick my gift for me?"

"That's precisely right young man.
You understand. That is the plan."

Grundle nodded his head and slightly winked one of his small, dark eyes to make the point.

"Be quiet, son," Calvin's mother whispered so Grundle wouldn't hear her.

"No, I won't be quiet!" Calvin shouted. "That's the dumbest thing I've ever heard. I don't like it one bit."

"I think it sounds kind of fun," a smart girl named Megan said.

"I think it's exciting," her friend Logan chipped in.

"Me too," said Nicole. "Think of the new friends we can make."

"Well, I'm just not going to play this silly game," said a spoiled girl named Karen. "See if I care if Santa doesn't give me a gift this year. My daddy will buy me anything I want."

"Don't be too sure, smarty," Karen's dad piped in. "I think Grundle's idea has possibilities. If you're not willing to have someone else choose for you, maybe it's better that you don't get any gifts at all for Christmas this year." She could tell he wasn't kidding.

Obviously, Karen's dad had great faith in Santa's judgment, and Grundle seemed to appreciate that kind of support from a wise grown-up. But Karen grumped sourly.

"Whose side are you on anyway?" she snipped, shooting a dirty look at her scowling dad.

"Well, I'm all for it," said Tamara excitedly.

"Me too," Susan and Evan said together. They were the obedient ones who never caused any trouble. They were always willing to do whatever they could to make people happy and win new friends.

"It's absolutely the most stupid thing I ever heard," Derik grumbled.

"I think it stinks!" said Jordan, but she didn't like anything anyone else wanted to do anyway. Neither did the twins, Alvin and Calvin. All they liked to do was push over snowmen.

The parents of the grumpy children were embarrassed, to say the least, but this wasn't the first time such a thing had happened. They didn't know what to do, except to hope that some day their children would grow up and learn to be nice.

Grundle stayed calm through it all. The kids had reacted the way he expected they would. But Santa had made it clear: if the kids of

Golden Cove wanted gifts from him this year, they had to do it his way, or not at all. There was no question about it. While this was an extremely uncommon thing for Santa to do, Grundle knew he must have felt the lesson was worth it. Santa had warned Grundle the grumpy kids would complain, but he also knew they would come around. They were not about to pass up their Christmas gifts this year. Santa knew little kids very well.

Grundle continued:

> "We'll start the giving right away,
> If you will be so kind,
> But let me tell you something else
> Ere you make up your mind.
>
> "The kids you're choosing these gifts for
> Live clear around the world.
> Their names are printed on this list;
> The scroll is thus unfurled."

From beneath his coat, Grundle pulled a small scroll that lengthened like a telescope as he pulled it out to at least four times its original size. His magic tricks were amazing enough, but what followed was even more interesting.

Everyone's eyes went to the scroll. There, printed in bold letters were some pretty strange names. Here's how it read:

The children of the village of Evoc Nedlog:

Boys:		Girls:	
	Kired		Nerak
	Nivla		Nadroj
	Nevets		Aramat
	Nivlac		Nagem
	Nagol		Elocin
	Nave		Nasus

Grundle continued:

"Though, sure, it's true their names are strange,
They're just like kids you know.
If that's not so the world around,
Then my father's name's not Bruno."

As the kids and their parents read the strange names of the village and its children, again there was a murmur throughout the group, followed by giggling in the back and an exclamation that sounded a lot like "He's gotta be kidding!"

"You've fifteen minutes, that is all
The time you have to talk.
I must be getting back to work.
And it is quite a walk!

"No coaching from the grown-ups, please.
This work is for the young.
When you hear the big bell sound,
Then kindly hold your tongue."

While the grown-ups chattered with amusement and gathered about Grundle to pepper him with questions, the children huddled at the edge of the square. Every one of them had something to say, and some of them said it loudly.

"This is the most ridiculous thing that has ever happened to me," Derik shouted. If I can't choose my own gift, I'm going to give whoever is at the other end something really dumb."

"Me too!" shouted Alvin. "We didn't ask to play this silly game."

"No!" cried Megan. "Those are children in a far away place. They're just like we are, and they'll probably do the best they can for us. I'm going to choose something really special for my person."

"Oh, me too," said Nicole. "I'll bet my person chooses something nice for me."

"That's a bunch of baloney!" Steven booed. "With names like that, how could they possibly know what we want? They're probably too dumb to even know what's good. I'll bet they would be happy to get a lump of coal."

"Now come on," Logan tried to reason. "After all, it's Santa's idea. He wouldn't be doing something that would hurt us or make us feel bad—unless we deserved it, of course. You guys can do whatever you want to do, but I'm going to choose the best thing I can think of for my person."

"So am I," Tamara said firmly. "You should love everybody, and how can you do something mean to someone you love?"

"I agree," Susan added. "That little girl around the world is counting on me. I'm not going to let her down."

"Well, not me," said Alvin. "That's not a very big bag, and maybe there aren't enough good gifts to go around. If we choose nice things for those other kids, there might not be any left for us. Calvin and I are going for something dumb, right Cal?"

"You bet," Calvin added. "What a great chance to pull a good joke on somebody. Those other kids don't know us. What difference will it make? Besides, if Santa can be so mean to us, why can't we be mean to them?"

It was clear there wasn't going to be any agreement among the children. They were as different as chocolate ice cream is from vanilla. The angry kids shouted and made ugly faces, but the agreeable ones had made up their minds to play the rules and pick out good gifts for the other kids.

As the noise rose to a roar, Grundle cut short a comment he was making to the grown-ups about how his magic bag was so heavy he was going to have to get reindeers to lug it around for him. He slammed the hammer down hard on the big brass bell.

Gong! Gong! Gong! Gong!

The noise ended quickly.

After talking with Grundle, all the grown-ups had smiles on their faces. They made room for the children to come to the front. Grundle invited all twelve children to stand beside him and his big box in a line. He had them face the crowd and told them to announce their choices in loud, clear voices so everyone could hear. Santa's magic bag would do the rest.

The kids silently took their places. Some were gloomy and some were happy. The moment of truth had arrived.

"I'll call your names out one by one.
Then tack upon your clothes
A little sign that tells the name
Of the one for whom you chose.

"Remember, choose it carefully,
The best that you can do.
Select the gift that you would like
For them to choose for you."

Silence filled the village square as Grundle read the first name.

"Derik first will play the game.
What gift for Kired will you name?"

Derik didn't even bat an eyelash, but an impish grin spread accross his face.

"A big, black lump of coal," he smirked. The grown-ups gasped, and half of the children giggled.

Grundle didn't say a word. His boney fingers fumbled with the scroll and pulled, and the name of Kired peeled from it like skin off a sunburned back. He placed it, along with another tag that said Evoc Nedlog, on Derik's chest right below his chin. The tags stuck firmly.

"Tamara now will play the game.
What gift for Aramat will you name?"

Tamara boldly stuck out her chin. "This is so exciting," she said. "I choose a pretty doll and a lovely house with all the furniture for her to live in," she said proudly.

The grown-ups cheered, and Grundle's fingers again went to the scroll. Aramat's name and the name of her village were placed on Tamara's chest.

And so it went.

Raunchy little Alvin chose a rusty, old tin can for Nivla.

Megan was very sweet. She watched Grundle closely as she chose a real pony with a pink saddle and all the trimmings for Nagem, because she would like one of those for herself.

And can you believe it, Steven chose a piece of used bubble gum for Nevets. The mean kids thought that was funny. They cheered loudly and patted him on the back.

Nicole chose generously for Elocin. She picked a closet full of pretty dresses.

Karen pulled a mean trick on Nerak. She chose a sink full of dirty dishes.

Logan thought hard about what he would like. He finally chose a talking computer for his new pal, Nagol. He hoped it was just the right thing.

Jordan laughed so hard that tears ran down her cheeks when all the grown-ups nearly passed out because she chose a live snake for the little girl named Nadroj.

Susan chose a beautiful ring with real diamonds and a plate of

chocolate chip cookies. She smiled at the thought of how pleased the little girl named Nasus would be with that kind of gift.

Calvin chose a popped balloon for Nivlac, which was even worse than his terrible habit of tipping over snowmen.

Evan chose a new mountain bike with a horn and a bell for Nave. Such a nice gift for a little boy he didn't even know!

Each time a gift was announced, Santa's magic bag bulged and shifted and made funny noises. The grown-ups either cheered or moaned, depending on what the children picked. It was hard to tell whether the nice kids or the naughty kids felt the best about their choices, because they all grinned as they thought about the impact they would have on the children in Evoc Nedlog.

The noisy discussion was again interrupted by the *Gong! Gong! Gong! Gong!* of the big brass bell, and once again everyone gave their attention to Grundle.

"The gifts have all been chosen,
And the names have been attached.
Now let's see the other side
And how the gifts are matched."

Grundle reached to his side and unfastened the small pouch. His hand reached inside as he said,

"Now here I have an object
That was made for this event.
It'll show you who's received your gift,
As well as what *they* sent.

"Cause it's a magic window
Where you can take a peek,
And look completely 'round the world
At that for which you seek."

Grundle pulled from the pouch a strange item that looked like a huge, wooden lollipop with a short handle and a fancy brass trim.

He handed it to Logan, who stood closest to him. Logan turned it over in his hands and examined it with great interest.

"Just hold it, lad. Don't let it drop.
There's one for each of you.
When all of you are holding one,
I'll tell you what to do."

One by one, each child received one of the magic windows. It was strange, but every time Grundle pulled a magic window out of the tight-fitting pouch, another one instantly took its place. Finally, every child held one of the curious objects. They waited anxiously for their instructions. Their hearts began to pound with excitement. They could only imagine what it would be like to look into a magic window that would allow them to see all the way around the world. The grown-ups murmured excitedly.

"Old Santa's bag is programmed,
And the choices all recorded.
As the windows open up,
The gifts will be awarded."

Santa's bag shuddered and shook. No one doubted that the bag was ready to do whatever was necessary in this strange game.

All of the children were growing aware that this was serious. The gift choices they had made were really going to be delivered. Some would probably even admit that they were beginning to feel sorry for the selections they had made, but it was too late now. Every eye shifted nervously between Grundle, the magic windows, and of course, Santa's bag.

"I hope whoever chose for me picked something really neat," Alvin excitedly whispered to his brother, Calvin. He'd already forgotten about the tin can he'd ordered for the poor kid at the other end of the game.

Grundle pulled another magic window from the pouch. He used this one to demonstrate.

"All right my friends, the time has come.
The bag is set and primed.
It's critical for what comes next
To be precisely timed.

"You'll notice on the very edge,
The windows have a hinge.
The latch is on the other side.
Of all the window's fringe.

"Now with your left hand, find the latch.
Your right will hold it steady.
As soon as you have got a hold,
Please holler that you're ready."

"Ready!" they all shouted as their fingers found the latches.

"I will count. You'll pop the lid
When you hear me say three.
One . . . two . . . three. Now open up
And shout out what you see."

With one quick, excited motion, every child's hand flipped a wooden cover, and all the children's eyes peered into a magic window. Every grown-up's eyes grew wide with anticipation, and every person held his or her breath.

It took a second for reality to strike. Then there were screams and yells among the children; some were screams of joy, and some were screams of sorrow. Some kids clasped their magic windows and looked again, just to be sure. Some threw their windows into the air or on the ground in a display of temper and frustration. Calvin even slammed his to the ground and stomped on it.

"This is no magic window," he said. "What kind of a stupid joke is this anyway?"

"This is crazy," Alvin cried. "It's a mirror! What's going on around here?"

"Oh, it's wonderful!" Megan said in excitement. "I can't believe it's really happening!"

The "magic windows" *were* mirrors. And when looked at in those fancy looking glasses, the printed village name of Evoc Nedlog became Golden Cove; Kired became Derik; Nivla became Alvin; and Nevets became Steven. And so it went. It was clear that each of the children were sending the chosen gifts to themselves.

Grundle shouted over the commotion:

"The windows did look 'round the world,
Their images quite clear.

Their view went clear around the world
And ended up right here."

The children either jumped with delight or stomped with fury. They knew everything that had been done was no one's fault or credit but their own, and it was almost more than some of them could handle.

The parents already knew what was going to happen because of their visit with Grundle. They laughed and slapped each other on the back. Then they laughed some more. Never had they had more Christmas fun. Even Grundle's face cracked an ever-so-slight smile.

Soon a strange, humming sound came from Santa's bag and began to rise above the chatter of the people.

The bag began to vibrate, then to jiggle, and then to wildly hop around. Sparks flew, whistles whistled, and sirens screamed. All of a sudden, the bag burst open, and there were ponies, kitchen sinks, dresses, dolls, tin cans, and snakes flying through the air.

People ducked and dodged. Trails of magic sparks carrying the gifts took off in all directions to the homes of the children. Each gift went to the home of the child who had chosen it, and landed right beside or underneath his or her Christmas tree with a thump!

Finally, the fury in Santa's magic bag fizzled out, and it slumped silent and empty to the ground. Grundle hopped down from his perch on the box. He placed the hammer and the big brass bell back into the smoldering bag.

Grundle sighed heavily with relief. He pulled a red handkerchief from his pocket and wiped his forehead with it. He looked weary, but pleased. He mumbled to the grown-ups nearest him to wish everyone a merry Christmas and asked them to tell the children that Santa loved them more than they could ever know. The lesson had been harsh for some of them, but he knew they would be better kids because of it. And because of that, this village would be the first on Santa's Christmas Visit List for next year.

He then left a message from Santa to the parents of certain children. Santa hoped they would not be too upset with him, but he was sure this event would help their families far more than it would hurt them. No parent was ever heard to disagree.

Then, without saying another word, Grundle stuffed himself into Santa's magic bag, pulled the strings tight, and POOF! All that was left was a small puff of white smoke and a slight odor that smelled like freshly baked gingerbread.

About the Author

Ted Collins Hindmarsh was born and raised in Provo, Utah. He is married to Shirlene Rasmussen, also from Provo. They have two daughters and three sons and a growing number of grandchildren and great-grandchildren.

Ted holds two degrees from Brigham Young University—a BS in print journalism and an MA in educational communication. After forty-four years of full-time service, he retired from BYU, where his career included Educational Media Services, Learning Resource Centers, the Freshman Academy program, and the Honor Code Office. He was also an adjunctive faculty member of the BYU Communications Department for thirty-five years.

After becoming an Eagle Scout, Ted was awarded the Silver Beaver for his service in scouting. He has held a variety of church and community youth leadership positions, including Cubmaster, Scoutmaster, youth mentor, and LDS bishop.